WESTFIELD MEMORIAL LIBRARY
WESTFIELD, NEW JERSEY

HUNKY DORY
ATE IT

To Jerry, Julie, and Chris
K.E.

For Lynn, Paula, David, Brenda,
and Rebel
J.M.S.

WESTFIELD MEMORIAL LIBRARY
WESTFIELD, NEW JERSEY

HUNKY DORY ATE IT

by Katie Evans
pictures by
Janet Morgan Stoeke

Dutton Children's Books
New York

J
Eva

Clara Lake
baked a cake.

Hunky Dory ate it.

Kate Donetti
boiled spaghetti.

Hunky Dory ate it.

Julie Fry
made a pie.

Hunky Dory ate it.

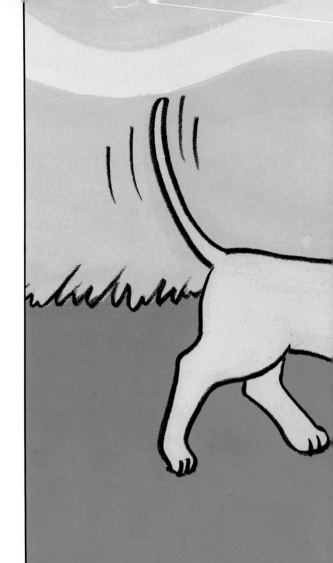

Sandy Drake
grilled a steak.

Hunky Dory ate it.

Mr. Hart
baked a tart.

Hunky Dory ate it.

Hunky Dory's
stomach dragged.
His sturdy tail
no longer wagged.

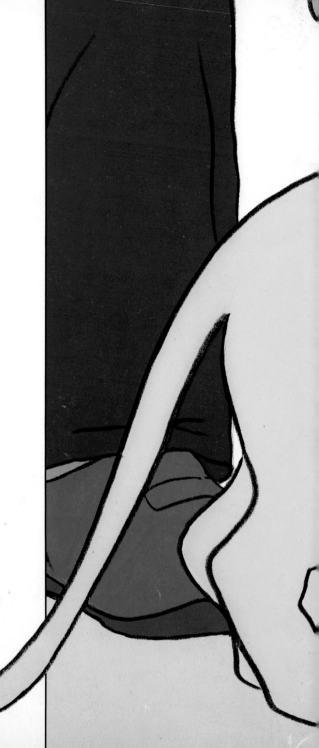

Julie found
her naughty pet.
She quickly took
him to the vet.

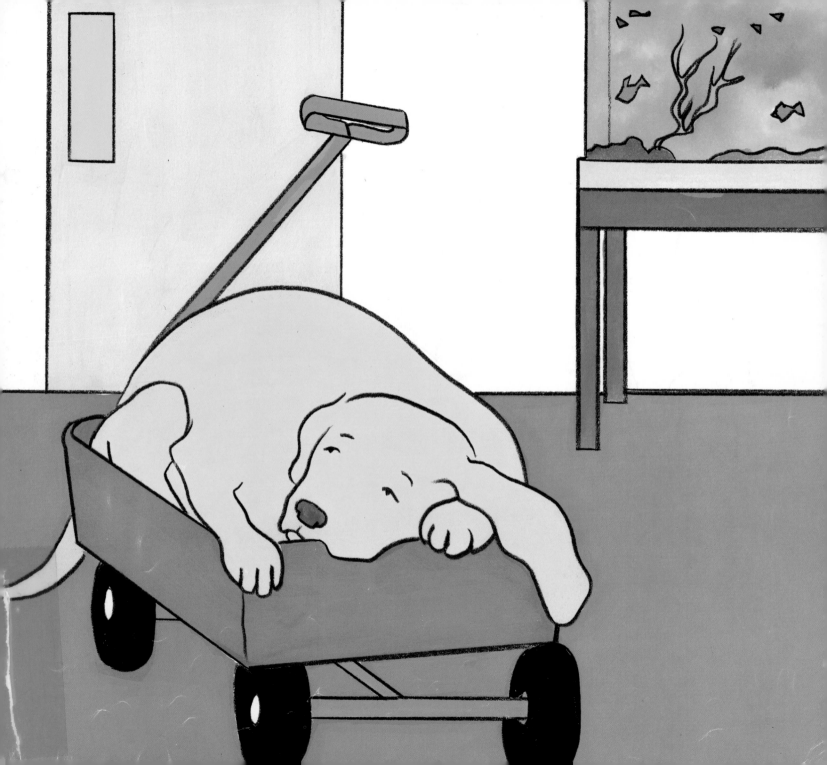

Dr. Phelp
had to help.

Hunky Dory
ate it.

WESTFIELD MEMORIAL LIBRARY
WESTFIELD, NEW JERSEY

2264991

Hunky Dory hated it.

WESTFIELD MEMORIAL LIBRARY
WESTFIELD, NEW JERSEY

Text copyright © 1992 by Katie Evans
Illustrations copyright © 1992 by Janet Morgan Stoeke
All rights reserved.

Library of Congress Cataloging-in-Publication Data
Evans, Katie.
Hunky Dory ate it/by Katie Evans; illustrated by Janet Stoeke.
p.   cm.
Summary: Spunky Hunky Dory tries to eat everything in sight—and
winds up a sick puppy at the vet's.
ISBN 0-525-44847-0
[1. Dogs—Fiction.   2. Food habits—Fiction.   3. Stories in rhyme.]
I. Stoeke, Janet Morgan, ill.   II. Title.
PZ8.3.E9Hu 1992
[E]—dc20
91-13992   CIP   AC

Published in the United States by Dutton Children's Books,
a division of Penguin Books USA Inc.
375 Hudson Street
New York, NY 10014
Designer: Riki Levinson
Printed in Hong Kong by South China Printing Co.
First Edition   10 9 8 7 6 5 4 3 2 1

WESTFIELD MEMORIAL LIBRARY

3 9550 00226 4991

WESTFIELD MEMORIAL LIBRARY
WESTFIELD, NEW JERSEY

J PICTURE Eva
Evans, Katie.
Hunky Dory ate it /

NOV 94